I'm a Wimp!

By **Jack Gabolinscy**

Illustrated by **Simon Bosch**

Rigby

I'm a Wimp!

My name is Jordan. I'm a wimp. I've always been a wimp and I always will be. Even now, on vacation with my friend Peta and her grandpa, I'm a wimp. I nearly drowned a few minutes ago. If I had, it would have been my own fault. I shouldn't ever try to be daring. I should stick to the things I'm good at, like reading and writing, dancing and singing, and performing on stage.

synonym:

A synonym is a word that means the same or nearly the same as another word.

Which word is the synonym for **wimp**?

A   champion
B   coward
C   pioneer

A, B, or C?

Peta and I were swimming in the river. Her grandpa told us to stay in the bigger, slower area. We did for a while. It was fun splashing and tipping each other off our tubes. But after a while, Peta got bored. "What else can we do?" she asked.

Some kids came rocketing down the river, laughing and shouting madly on tubes and rafts. They shot off down the rapids, around the corner, and out of sight. They were having a great time. "Come on," said Peta. "Let's follow them."

I knew we shouldn't, but . . . I looked over at her grandpa. He was still sitting on his rock where he could see us, but he was talking to a woman and patting her dog.

"Come on then," I agreed.

"Let's go."

Question:

Why do you think the narrator was reluctant to follow the kids?

rocketing down the river

We climbed into our tubes and paddled out to the fast-moving current. Soon we were shooting the rapids, laughing and shouting hysterically, like the other kids.

It was fun bouncing along like buoys in a stormy bay. You couldn't fight against the current in the white water, but by kicking or paddling with your hands, you could steer closer to the bank or further out to the middle. But then the river got wider, rougher, and shallower. Our knees and feet banged painfully on the bottom. I didn't like it.

Even Peta was a bit worried.

Simile or Metaphor?

... like buoys in a stormy bay

A simile compares one thing to another by using the words "like" or "as", and often creates a mental picture in the reader's mind.

A metaphor compares one thing to another without using the words "like" or "as", and often creates a mental picture in the reader's mind.

Suddenly, as we spun around a bend, we smashed into a half-submerged rock. Our tubes flew out from under us and we were left out of control and unsupported. My face went under. I panicked.

"Help! Help!"

"Help!" I screamed, as the wild water rolled me head-over-heels, like a pair of pants in the washing machine. "Help!" I spluttered, grabbing desperately for something to hold.

Every time I screamed, I sank under the water and came up spluttering and splashing, more panicky than before.

I thought I was going to drown. I really did.

Problem:	Solution:
No tubes for support	?

How do you think the problem could be solved?

9

Then suddenly, my feet hit the bottom. At the same time, a man grabbed me. "Here, hold my hand!" he shouted. "You're OK." He helped me back onto the shore. I was shaking and embarrassed. The man had saved my tube, too. "Feel better now?" he asked.

I did feel better, and you would think I would be thankful. But no — not me. I felt more embarrassed than thankful. I went into shock. "No!" I whimpered. "Oh, no! I hate it." I don't know what I hated, but that's what I shouted.

Clutching the tube in both hands, I started running. Crying and running, stumbling and tripping, sobbing and sniffling, back along the river bank I went. I was scared and embarrassed and ashamed.

Question:

"Oh, no! I hate it." I don't know what I hated, but that's what I shouted.

What do you think the narrator really hated?

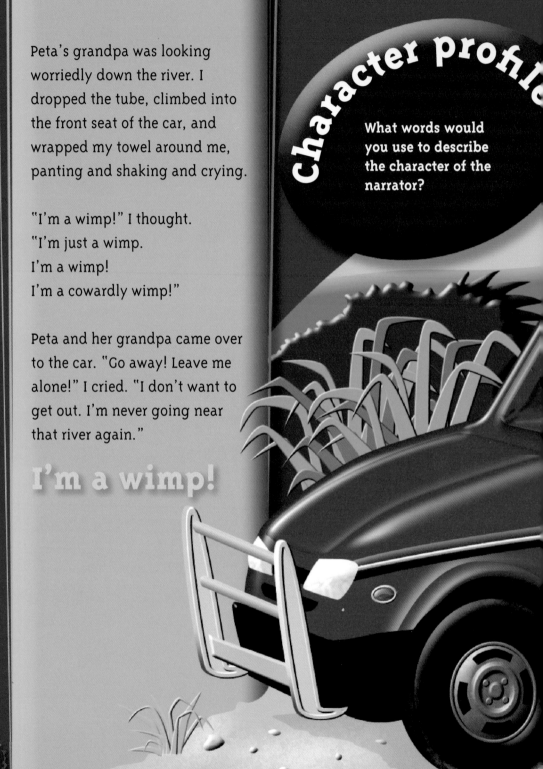

Peta's grandpa was looking worriedly down the river. I dropped the tube, climbed into the front seat of the car, and wrapped my towel around me, panting and shaking and crying.

"I'm a wimp!" I thought.
"I'm just a wimp.
I'm a wimp!
I'm a cowardly wimp!"

Peta and her grandpa came over to the car. "Go away! Leave me alone!" I cried. "I don't want to get out. I'm never going near that river again."

I'm a wimp!

Character profile

What words would you use to describe the character of the narrator?

That's the way it always is. If I try to do anything just a little bit different – a little bit daring – I fail. Even when I was a little kid, it was like that.

Once, when I was five, I went to the mall with Mom. I kept seeing things I wanted to look at.

"Hold my hand," said Mom.

It was like being on a dog leash. Every time I tried to go and see something, Mom's arm pulled me back. When Mom let go of my hand to buy something, I was off like a dog off the leash. I didn't mean to go anywhere. It just happened.

like a dog

Action	Response
Mom let go my hand	?

off the leash

15

I ran like a dog hunting a bone. I looked at some bright red shoes in one store. Then I saw a two-wheeler bike. I ran across to look at that. An ice-cream shop caught my eye, and off I went to investigate. Everywhere I turned, there were more exciting things to see and do.

Next thing I knew, I was lost. I looked around, and all I could see were strange faces. Strange faces, strange voices, and strange places!

I panicked. I stood there and opened my mouth wide like a barn door.

"Aaaaaahhhh! Aaaaaahhhh! Aaaaaahhhh!"

It sounds funny now, but it wasn't funny at the time. So you see, even then I was a wimp.

Aaaaa

I was a wimp just two days ago, when we went horseback riding. I was super-excited, and it was great until we came to a bridge across the river. A dog barked at a bird in the grass. My horse got spooked and bolted.

Imagine **me**, screaming over the paddock, my feet sticking out in all directions! **Me** losing the reins and holding the saddle! **The dog**, running along beside us, barking as if was great fun! **The horse** running and skipping like a wild thing!

Peta and the horse's owner just laughed. I wanted to get off, and I would have, but I was too embarrassed. Instead, I stayed on and rode another thirty minutes across the hills and over that same bridge again. I suppose it was fun . . . but it was scary when the horse took off.

Inference:

What inferences can you make about what Peta and the horse's owner thought when they laughed at the narrator?

19

And then again, yesterday, I behaved like a wimp when we went bungy jumping. I watched everybody else jumping off. They were getting so psyched! I couldn't wait for my turn. Then the girl tied the straps around my ankles. I looked down at the water and rocks below. I got scared. My heart started thumping. My face got all hot. "Wait!" I said to the girl. "Wait!" Every time she started counting to ten . . . "Wait!"

"Wait!"

clarify the term:
"getting so psyched"

I looked at all the people. They all thought I was a wimp. I could tell by their faces. I knew I *had* to jump. But when I looked over the side, I got scared again.

In the end, I did jump. It was great. It's the best thing I've ever done.

Pretty good for a wimp!

Now Peta and her grandpa want me to go back in the river.

No way!

"I'm never going in there again. I'm never swimming in a river. Go away and leave me alone! I'm a wimp. I am. I'm a wimp."

Question:

Why do you think the narrator said he could tell by the people's faces that they thought he was a wimp?

I'm a wimp!

23

Peta doesn't agree. "You're not a wimp," she says. (She's sure to say that — she's my friend.) Her grandpa doesn't think I'm a wimp, either. "You're one of the bravest kids I know," he said.

He's just being nice. He's always like that.

Finally I agree to get out of the car and sit in the sun to dry off. After a few minutes, I feel a bit better. "Maybe I will just sit on the edge here in the shallow water."

Question:

Why do you think Grandpa said the narrator was "one of the bravest kids I know"?

And you guessed it, now I'm all the way back in the water. Peta and I are splashing around in our tubes. Her grandpa's sitting on the stone again, watching us. But we're not leaving the calm area this time. Oh no!

I wish I wasn't such a wimp. It's awful being a coward.

It's been a neat vacation. We've done all sorts of fun things. Rock climbing, river rafting, bungy jumping, jetski riding, horseback riding, mini-car racing, and bumper boating.

It's going to be sad when we go home tomorrow. Still, we're stopping on the way to go jetski riding again, and I think we're going to another bungy jump place. I can't wait to do it again.

"I wish I wasn't such a wimp, though."

Character profile:

What words do you think best describe the character of the narrator?

coward   kind

wimp

caring   brave   inquisitive

daring   bold

insecure

26

Think about the text

Making connections – talk about the connections you can make to the story *I'm a Wimp!*

being brave

being nervous

having self-confidence

feeling fear

Text-to-Self

meeting failure

having supportive friends

needing encouragement

Text-to-Text

Talk about other stories you may have read that have similar features. Compare the stories.

Text-to-World

Talk about situations in the world that might connect to elements in the story.

Planning a Short Story

1 **Decide on a storyline**

Jordan, the main character, thinks he's a wimp.	He and his friend, Peta, go swimming in the river, and get into fast water.	Jordan panics and has to be rescued.
Jordan is embarrassed and thinks back to other times when he behaved like a wimp.	Grandpa and Peta encourage Jordan to face the river again.	Jordan overcomes his fear and goes back into the river, although he still thinks he is a wimp.

2 **Think about the characters**

Think about the way they will think, act, and feel.
Make some short notes or quick sketches.

Jordan	Peta	Grandpa

afraid nervous scared	fun-loving enthusiastic curious	understanding supportive helpful

③ Decide on the setting or settings

Make some short notes.

④ Decide on the events in order

Introduction

Events

Conclusion

Short stories usually have . . .

A A short introduction that grabs the reader's interest

B Fewer characters than longer stories

C A single fast-moving plot

D A climax that occurs late in the story